The Warmint

a poem by Walter de la Mare

The Warmint

illustrated by EVALINE NESS

Charles Scribner's Sons   New York

To Matthew, Mark, and Carey:
warmints all.

Oh, she was just a little thing
    A slim thing, a narrow thing,
    A pig-tailed, dark and black-eyed thing,
    Not five span.

She didn't care a fig, a fig,
For any creature, small or big
Gander, turkey, cow or pig—

WOMAN OR MAN.

She set papa a booby-trap,
It tumbled on his head.

She dived into the water-butt.

Lit fireworks in the shed.

The bed they call an apple-pie
  She made poor cook for Sunday—

Played with the bunnies under the moon
Through half the night to Monday.

Oh, she was just a little thing,
A starry, dark, mischievous thing,
An imp of mischief, out and in,
A terror, tax and torment.
Mamma called her her precious lamb...

Cook cooked her custards, tarts and flam.

The gardener, whose name was Sam,
Wild strawberries grew to make her jam.

Oh, she was just a little thing
    A slim thing, a narrow thing,
    A pig-tailed, dark and black-eyed thing,
    Not five span.
    The nurse who wheeled her in her pram,
    And stitched her many a garment,
    No peace a moment ever knew.

And yet they loved her through and through—

THIS WICKED LITTLE WARMINT.

Walter de la Mare's poetry is well known to all those who love children's books, as is the spirited art of Evaline Ness.